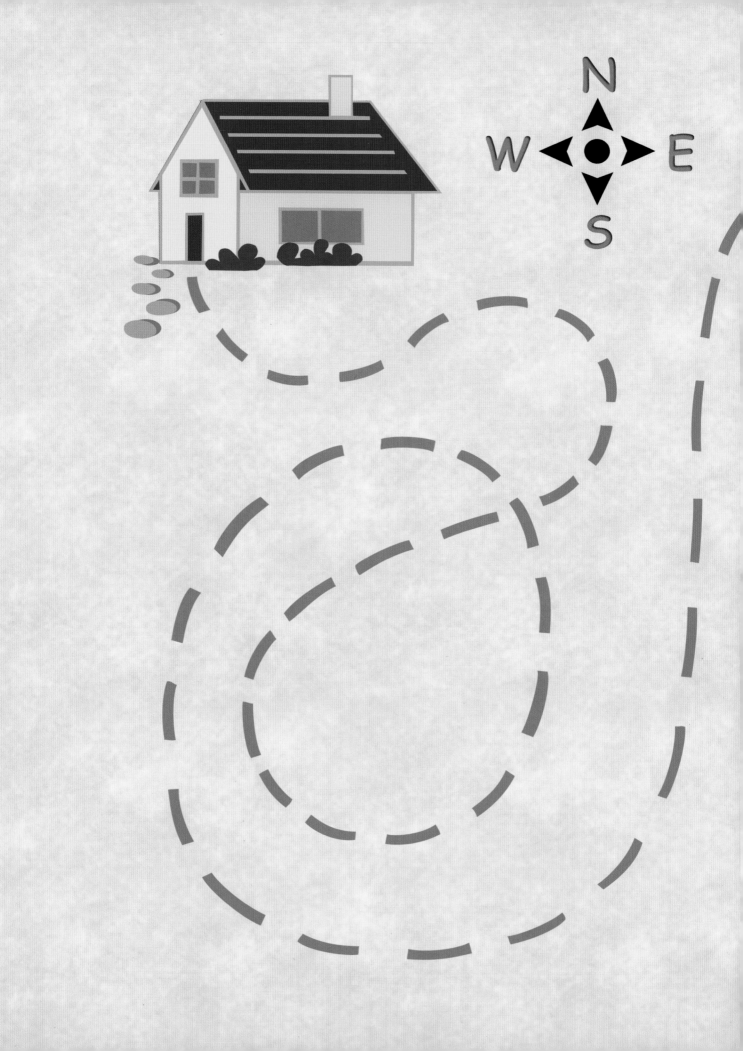

The Parts We Play
10th reprint ©2017
by Michael Jr.

Published by Michael Jr. Productions
Copyright (c) 2008-2017 Michael Jr. Productions
Illustrations (c) 2008-2017 Michael Jr. Productions
www.michaeljr.com

ISBN 978-0-615-14175-6

Dedicated to:
Anyone who thinks they don't
play an important part.

Special thanks to two amazing parents,
an awesome wife and five great kids.

Much Thanks to:
ERIC THOMPSON

Printed in China

THE PARTS WE PLAY

2nd Edition

by Michael Jr.

Illustrated by

Yalisa T. Carter

One Saturday morning, little Gracie woke up very excited. This wasn't like any regular Saturday. *This* Saturday was the one she had been waiting for, for quite some time. This was the day her dad was taking her to her favorite place to have fun - Jr. Island!

Gracie was so excited, she got dressed and ready to go *extra* early. She could hardly wait to get in the car. She grabbed her tickets as she said to her dad, "Daddy! Daddy! Today is the day! Can we go to Jr. Island now?"

"Okay, okay. Let's get ready to go", her dad happily replied. "Your mother has already made our lunches and we are all set for an exciting day at Jr. Island - just Daddy and his little girl."

Not long after breakfast, they got in the car and were ready to go. Once they buckled their seat belts, Gracie waved goodbye to her mom and they were on their way to Jr. Island.

After they had been driving awhile, Gracie and her dad felt the car shake and heard a strange sound coming from the car.

"What was that?" asked Gracie. "I'm not really sure," her dad replied. "I hope everything is alright, Daddy..." "I'm sure it'll be just fine, Honey."

Just then, the car made that same strange noise and started to shake again. "I'd better try to find out what's going on," said Gracie's dad as he pulled the car over to the side of the road.

"What are we going to do Daddy?" "I'm going to get out and take a look. You stay here, Sweetheart. I'll be right back." Gracie's dad got out and opened the hood. "Okay, what seems to be the problem here?" he said.

Man, I do too much of the work around here. I am exhausted! said Muffler
What are you talking about? I am the one getting worn out. Look at me, I'm TIRED! said Wheely
Then Battery said, Be quiet, be quiet!! I'm in charge, I'm in charge and everyone should listen to me.

With that said, they all agreed to switch jobs to see if it would make things better for everyone. All except Radiator, that is, who was still trying to keep things cool ...

Gracie's dad tries to start the car again, but nothing happens.

While they are arguing, Wheely hears something coming from inside the car. Tears began to stream down Gracie's face when she saw that now, the car wouldn't even start.

As all the parts stood there listening, they heard the Father speak. "Why don't you just do what I need you to do? I give you everything you need, I never put you through more than you can stand, I take good care of you and I always keep you covered and protected. Why won't you just do what I need you to do?"

Look, being important doesn't do anyone any good if we don't work together. Battery, having a charge is only important, if you use it to help activate Starter. Fuely, if you and Sparky don't work together, Rodney won't have any energy to help put Wheely and the others into motion. And Muffler, we need you to keep things clean and quiet while I make sure no one gets too hot. We're each made to do something that no one else can do and we all need each other in order to truly play our parts, said Radiator

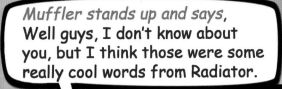

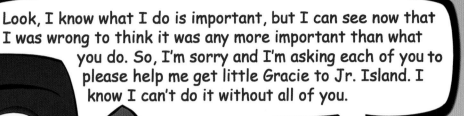

Quickly, they all ran to their places, but it looked like they were too late. A tow truck had pulled up in front of the car to take it away. If this happened, Gracie would not be able to go to Jr. Island.

Before the tow truck driver hitched the car, something told Gracie's dad to try and start the car once more.

Slowly, he twisted the key one final time and the car started with great ease! Gracie cheered with excitement!

Just to be sure, the tow truck driver checked the parts and said, "It must have been a little glitch. These things happen sometimes. You can head on your way now. I looked over all the parts and everything is working very well."

So Gracie and her dad went to Jr. Island and had lots of fun with rides, shows and lots of cotton candy - just as they had planned! Everything worked out perfectly as it always does when we all play our parts.

What Part Do You Play?